JUAN BOBO AND THE PIG

A PUERTO RICAN FOLKTALE RETOLD BY FELIX PITRE

ILLUSTRATED BY CHRISTY HALE

LODESTAR BOOKS

DUTTON   NEW YORK

to the memory of my *abuelo* (grandfather),
Magdaleno Díaz, who, like me, was a
storyteller by nature and a child at heart

—F.P.

in memory of my brother, David Charles Hale

—C.H.

Library of Congress Cataloging-in-Publication Data
Pitre, Felix
  Juan Bobo and the pig: a Puerto Rican folktale/retold by Felix Pitre;
illustrated by Christy Hale.—1st ed.
    p.   cm.
  Summary: While his mother goes to church, Juan cares for the pig
with humorous results.
  ISBN 0-525-67429-2
  1. Juan Bobo (Legendary character)—Juvenile literature.
[1. Juan Bobo (Legendary character) 2. Folklore—Puerto Rico.]
I. Hale, Christy, ill.   II. Title.
PZ8.1.P683Ju   1993
398.21—dc20
[E]   92-28063
                                             CIP
                                             AC

Published in the United States by Lodestar Books,
an affiliate of Dutton Children's Books,
a division of Penguin Books USA Inc.,
375 Hudson Street, New York, New York 10014

Published simultaneously in Canada
by McClelland & Stewart, Toronto

Editor: Rosemary Brosnan   Designer: Christy Hale
Printed in Hong Kong   First Edition
10 9 8 7 6 5 4 3 2 1

FOREWORD

When I was young, my *abuelo,* my grandfather, told me a story about a boy who was very famous. This boy, Juan Bobo, was the folk hero of Puerto Rico. Everyone made fun of poor little Juan Bobo and said he was *un bobo,* a fool. But Juan's silly ways always led to a lesson that showed the so-called smart people that they, too, could act like him.

The tradition of the "wise" fool can be found in stories from many lands. In Puerto Rico, the significance of Juan Bobo is tied to the humorous wisdom of the country folk, or as they are better known, the *jíbaros.* The *jíbaro* was a product of many cultures—the native Taino, the African, and the Spaniard. In essence, he was the first true Puerto Rican, with a mystical tie to the land and a wary eye toward his European overlords. Juan Bobo stories were used by the *jíbaro* to expose the often pompous and silly behavior of the aristocratic Spanish rulers and those Puerto Ricans who imitated them.

My grandfather probably heard this Juan Bobo story from his parents or grandparents and, as is often the custom in Puerto Rico, added his own embellishments to it in the retelling. I, in turn, brought my own experience and training as an improvisational actor/storyteller and second generation Puerto Rican (or Nuyorican as we are sometimes known) to presenting this story in a bilingual format. Although I have added a couple of modern "improvements" such as a refrigerator and a soft drink, and enhanced the mother's dressing up (I don't recall my *abuelo* mentioning a girdle), the main idea of this Juan Bobo story remains the same. And that idea lies in the *jíbaro*'s gut feeling that what really matters is being honest, speaking truthfully, knowing who you are, and being content with that knowledge.

One day, Juan Bobo's mother called to her son, "Juan Bobo! *¿Donde estás?* Where are you? Juan Bobo!"
Juan Bobo heard his mother calling and came running to their small house, singing:

> *Mi nombre,* my name, is Juan Bobo!
> Juan means John,
> And I love my mom.
> *Mi nombre,* my name, is Juan Bobo!

"*Sí, Mami. ¿Qué tú quieres?* What do you want?" he
asked as he skipped happily into the house.

"Juan Bobo," answered his mother, "today is Sunday,
domingo, and I am going to church, to *la iglesia.*"

"Oh, yes, Mami. Today is Sunday, *domingo,* and you are
going to church, to *la iglesia.* What do you want me to do?"

"While I am gone, I want you to take good care of the
puerquito, the pig."

"Oh, yes, Mami. I'll take very good care of the *puerquito*," he said with a laugh. You see, the pig was Juan's favorite animal. Juan often spent hours playing with and talking to him.

"Bueno, good. Go and play now," Mami said. Then she went to her room to get dressed for church. First, Juan Bobo's mother put on her *faja,* her girdle. (Oh! It was a little tight.)

OHHH!

Next she put on her *vestido*, her dress. Then came her *aretes*, her earrings, and her *collares*, her necklaces. Finally she put on *brazaletes*, her many glittering bracelets. "There! I'm all ready to go to *la iglesia*," she said as she admired herself in the mirror. "Oh, Juan Bobo!"

aHHHH!

Hearing his mother calling him again, Juan Bobo skipped into the house. He was about to ask his mother what she wanted when the sight of her all dressed up in her fancy clothes and jewelry made him freeze in his tracks. With his mouth wide open, he stood there staring for a moment (although it seemed longer) and finally exclaimed, "Ooooo! *¡Mamacita! ¡Qué bonita!* How beautiful you look!"

His mother was very pleased to hear this but only managed a vain smile and replied "*Sí,* yes, I know." And reminding him to take good care of the *puerquito* while she was away, she gave him *un besito,* a kiss, and left for church.

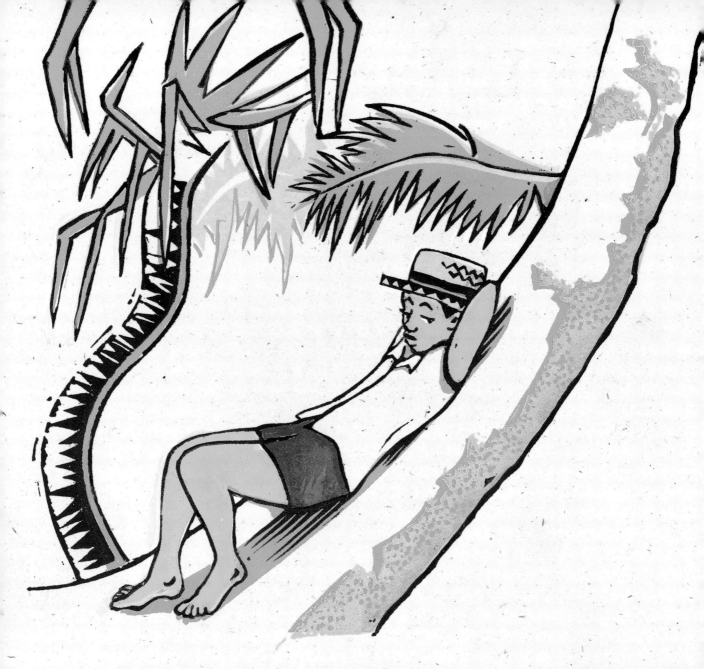

Ay, *qué bueno,* this is great, Juan thought. I have nothing to do but take it easy and relax. Suddenly, Juan heard…the pig. He was making so much noise. But you know, the pigs in Puerto Rico don't say "oink, oink." They go like this: "Chruuurh! Chruuurh!"

Juan Bobo ran outside, where he found the pig squealing in his pen. "*¿Qué pasa?* What's wrong?" he asked the pig.

The pig looked at Juan and said, "Chruuurh! Chruuurh!"

"I understand," answered Juan. "*Tú tienes hambre,* you're hungry."

So he dashed into the house, opened the refrigerator,
and grabbed something that looked good to him.

He rushed back to the pig and, giving him the food, said, "Here you are. I have brought you…*chuletas de cerdo*, pork chops!"

The pig looked at the pork chops and began to squeal much louder than before, "Chruuurh! Chruuurh!"

"Oh, you're not hungry, so…*tienes sed,* you're thirsty!"

Juan ran back into the house and searched the refrigerator again. When he went outside, he brought the pig...soda!

The *puerquito* sniffed the soda and began to squeal louder than ever, "CHRUUURH! CHRUUURH!"

"Oh, what could be wrong?" asked Juan Bobo. He ran around frantically as the pig kept squealing, "CHRUUURH! CHRUUURH!"

"I know, *yo se,* I know. You want to go to church with Mami!" But Juan Bobo looked at the pig and thought, he can't go to church like that. So Juan entered the pen, grabbed the squirming pig, and carried him inside to Mami's room.

First he put one of his mother's girdles on the pig.
The pig said, "Chruuurh?"

Next Juan put his mother's best dress on the pig.
The pig said, "Chruuurh??"

Then Juan put his mother's earrings, necklaces, and
bracelets on the pig. The pig said, "Chruuurh???"

"*Ahora,* now, you are ready for church!" Juan Bobo opened the door and let the pig go.

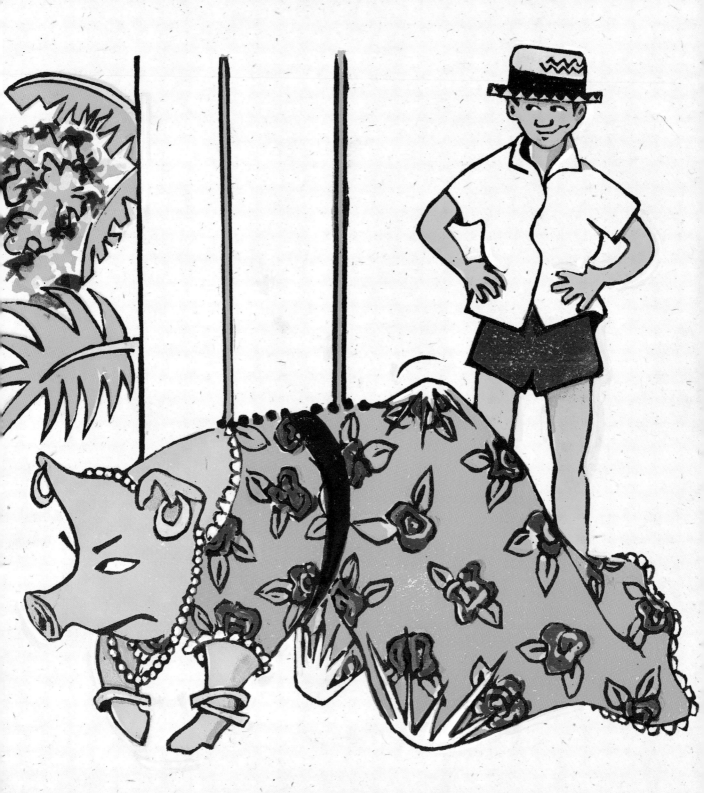

The *puerquito* ran outside, down the road, and jumped into the *fango*, the old mudhole!

A while later, Juan Bobo's mother came home. When she didn't see the pig in the pen or Juan Bobo in the house, she called her son's name.

Juan came running in and said, "Ah, Mami, did you have a good time at *la iglesia,* at church?"

"Never mind that," his mother replied. "Did you take good care of the *puerquito?*"

"Oh, Mami, I took good care of the *puerquito*. Yes, good care."

"But where is he? *¿Donde está?*" asked his mother.

"Well, he was upset and kept saying 'chruuurh, chruuurh,' so I dressed him up in your girdle and dress and jewelry and sent him to church! To *la iglesia!*" As Juan Bobo spoke, he saw his mother's expression change from her usual pleasant smile to a look of horror.

"*¿Qué, qué?* You did what?"

She ran outside, calling the *puerquito.* "Here, piggy, piggy, piggy! Here, piggy, piggy, piggy!" And there, in the MUD, wearing her GIRDLE, and her DRESS, and her JEWELRY was…the PIG! "Oh, my girdle, and my dress, and my jewelry…JUAN BOBO!"

And for about a week, Juan Bobo could not sit down. At least not without a pillow.

So to this day, in Puerto Rico, whenever a woman or a man dresses up with lots of fancy jewelry and fancy clothes, pretending to be someone he or she is not, people will say, "That person looks like *la puerca de Juan Bobo*," or Simple John's pig.

And that is the story of Juan Bobo!